FADE TO GREY

Edward M. Grant

Banchixi Media
Canada

First Edition, 2013

Paperback
ISBN-13: 978-1-927549-13-1

eBook
ISBN-13: 978-1-927549-12-4

Published by Banchixi Media, **www.banchixi.com**

CHAPTER ONE

It began the way these things usually do. Alarms blaring around the ship, and the organics screaming as they realize they're probably going to die. Normally, followed by a large explosion that confirms those fears.

Maintenance Bot M-3 had always been proud of the smooth and reliable operation of the starships it maintained, but a few hours idle, strapped into an uncomfortable power and data cradle in the *Tumbleweed*'s engineering section, was enough to start its manipulators twitching. They wanted to plunge into a desperate struggle against the forces of chaos and decay, while the ship and the organics inside it watched in hope and fear, knowing their very lives depended on a successful repair.

Rolling, it told the ship, when the call to action came through the internal maintenance Net.

It grabbed the nearest railing with a primary manipulator, and pulled itself from the cradle. The rapid movement triggered the emergency disconnect, and the cables from the cradle pulled free, twisting and turning behind it in microgravity.

It activated the warning lights on its back and sides as it twisted toward the hatch, then powered up the MHD fans on its sides to push itself out of the maintenance storage area. A brown-furred cat-girl squealed and pulled herself out of the way as M-3 flew through the hatch.

"Watch where you're going," she shouted as it passed inches above her ears.

Urgent repairs. No time to stop to apologize. The thrill of a desperate race against time with all eyes watching was what it lived for.

M-3 broadcast an emergency alert message over the Net, telling everyone on board to clear its route, then activated its siren and ran the fans up to full power. The cat-girl clung to the wall, out of the way, as M-3 accelerated to its top speed of three metres per second and blew past her.

Its orange warning lights flashed across the corridor walls as it flew toward area seven. Two synthetics in spider-like bodies clinging to the walls dodged out of the way, then M-3 twisted the fans sideways and flipped upside down near the ceiling to pass a crowd of organics heading for the observation deck. A few seconds later it spun the fans to full reverse, and reached out a primary manipulator to the nearest hand-hold on the wall.

The drink dispenser on C-deck had begun dispensing milk instead of apple juice again, and the organics wanted it fixed. M-3 hooked into the dispenser's maintenance port, and ran the diagnostics.

The HD 97950 shipyard had outfitted the *Tumbleweed* with the latest in food and drink assembler technology before it left, but they never worked worth a damn. Within six months, the ship's Synthetic Intelligence core had told the maintenance bots to rip them out and replace them with something more robust.

They never quite managed it.

One of the liquid selection valves had jammed open, so M-3 extracted the valve with a tertiary manipulator. Apple seeds were jammed into the bearings. It pulled out the seeds and stuffed them into its waste storage unit, then disassembled the valve for materials and began to assemble a replacement.

Hurry up, the *Tumbleweed*'s SI said over the Net.

"Warp drive shutdown in five seconds," it said over the ship's internal speakers.

I want all bots ready to carry out essential maintenance straight after shutdown, it added over the Net.

What was the point in hurrying to make a quick fix and having to do it all over again next week? Get it right the first time and it would work for years.

The organics were probably on the observation deck to watch the show as they arrived in the new system, but M-3 had seen it more than enough in the centuries it had spent in space, travelling on a dozen starships. Stars all look the same after a while. Big, small, blue, red, it was just another ball of hydrogen blasting light into space like a malfunctioning fusion reactor.

Except, when they do go wrong, they can't be repaired.

It pulled the new valve from the assembler with a tertiary manipulator, and grabbed the pipe with another. It measured pipe and valve with its laser scanner to ensure a good fit, then pushed the new valve toward the pipe.

The ship shuddered and shook, the pipe twisted in M-3's manipulator, and the valve missed the connection. Milliseconds later, alarms began to blare.

The ship creaked. M-3 adjusted its manipulators and slid the valve onto the pipe, then twisted it into place. An alarm came over the maintenance Net.

Then another. Then more.

SI Core Shutdown.

Reactor Output Zero.

Emergency Power Activated.

Internal Pressure Falling.

High Atmospheric Particulate Levels.

The *Tumbleweed* shook and twisted like a dying animal. It was out of power, the hull was leaking, something was on fire, and the SI core would be no help.

That just made M-3's day.

It tapped its manipulators together. Now it could really get into some serious repairs.

It powered up its fans, and grabbed the nearest railing with its manipulators to steady itself as the corridor swung from side to side and bangs and thuds filled the air. Two organics pulled themselves along the railing toward the stern, a human and the cat-girl. She wore a skinsuit, and swore as she tried to pull the helmet into place with one hand while holding a metal box about thirty centimetres across in the other.

The lights flashed and dimmed.

"Fix the ship," the cat-girl said.

"Just a minute," M-3 said as it locked the valve in place.

More alarms.

Habitat Section Vibration Outside Tolerance.

Emergency Power Excessive Drain.

Strain In Spine Approaching Critical Levels.

The safety systems were trying to brake the ship's rotating habitat sections with thrusters and gyros before the vibration broke the hull, and that was sucking up most of the emergency power. M-3 checked the location of the organics through the Net, but most of them seemed to be outside and moving away.

They might be abandoning the ship, but it wasn't.

First priority had to be power to bring the SI core online so it could decide how to proceed. M-3 twisted and turned in the air to avoid the organics and other bots blocking the vibrating corridor as it struggled through the engineering section toward the reactor. A vending machine squirted blobs of liquid into the air ahead and M-3 felt a strong urge to stop and repair it, but the reactor was still the highest priority.

It opened the reactor room entrance hatch and flew into the airlock which protected the rest of the ship from airborne radiation. The hatch on the far side was safety-locked, claiming the reactor room was in vacuum.

Organics might need to breathe, but M-3 didn't. It overrode the lock, vented the airlock and opened the hatch.

Stars.

All it could see through the open hatch were space, stars and a few spars and cables where the reactor room had been. Only then did it double-check the maintenance Net and discover the reason the reactor wasn't producing power was that it wasn't there any more.

The rear of the *Tumbleweed* was gone.

Where was it? M-3 scanned the dark space behind the ship and spotted something flashing in the distance, perhaps the rear of the ship tumbling through space a few kilometres behind them. Could it reach the reactor and repair the ship?

The numbers said it would take ten minutes to travel that far unless it burned a dangerous amount of thruster fuel, even if the rear wasn't moving away. And there was no way M-3 could push it back to reattach it.

Time to reprioritize repair tasks.

As it tried to determine any way to fix the ship without the reactor and SI core, a body floated in front of its optical sensors. One of the organics was out in space without a vac suit. M-3 felt an urge to grab them and take them back inside.

"Do your job and let them do theirs," the SI core had always said. M-3 followed its advice, and watched the organic tumble away into the dark shadow on the far side of the ship.

It needed the SI core online to tell it what to do. And it needed a working reactor to power the core. No other option.

Perhaps it could assemble a cable, attach that to the broken spars outside the airlock and to the rear of the ship, then pull it back? Then it could reattach them somehow.

The airlock walls shook. Then the airlock door smashed into M-3's back.

The walls bent and panels broke apart. M-3 tumbled into space, the habitation sections twisting and spinning behind it as the vibration snapped the ship's spine. Then the torn remnants of the counter-rotating habitation cylinders broke free. Brief bursts of flame blew out into space as they smashed into the side of the ship, until the flames went out as the air dissipated and the *Tumbleweed*'s hull snapped in a dozen places.

Now that was what M-3 called a repair job.

It span in the middle of the debris cloud until its thrusters killed the rotation. A chunk of hull thudded against its side and M-3 grabbed it. More passed ahead, and it took hold of as much as it could. ID tags showed it had found hull panels 3701A and 3700B. When oriented correctly, they still fit together where the ship's last struggles had torn them apart, and it held them while its nanomanipulators repaired the join at the molecular level. In moments, the panels were as good as new.

If it could just collect all the pieces of the ship together, M-3 could repair it. That would take a while, but the SI core and the organics would finally praise its skill and devotion when they were able to go back aboard and continue their trip. Perhaps not the organics floating stiffly among the debris, their frozen bodies tumbling in the vacuum of space, but certainly the ones who had abandoned the ship before it broke up.

Something thumped into M-3's back. A diamond-titanium composite girder from the ship's spine. It couldn't repair that without the other end of the girder, so it assembled a net, which it began to fill with any components it couldn't match up.

As it rotated, it saw where the orbit was taking them. Not far ahead was a planet, a spherical mass of grey and blue with a faint haze of white clouds above it.

M-3's thrusters would soon be out of fuel if it tried to collect all the debris in the cloud. It assembled another net on the end of a cable and began throwing that out to catch the nearest chunks of wreckage, making careful use of its internal gyros to stabilize itself as it pulled them in. Over the next hour, it accumulated a couple of tons, and reassembled a dozen hull panels. But the rest was floating away, into the depths of space.

And the planet was larger than it had been an hour before.

Much larger.

Blue lakes and rivers contrasted sharply against the dull, grey surface around them, but there was no hint of the greenery of a human habitat or colony. As M-3 continued to collect the wreckage, it passed over what could have been a human city with tall buildings reaching toward the sky, yet still grey with no green. The planet rotated beneath it, and the city moved into the twilight shadows, yet no lights turned on.

M-3 began to shake. Slowly and gently at first, but more rapidly as the planet grew larger. Its skin sensors warned that its external temperature was rising. The ground was closer and clearer than ever before, and the nearby debris began to tumble. Something pulled M-3 slowly away from the net, until the cable went tight.

Then everything began to burn.

CHAPTER TWO

M-3 rebooted in the dark, with its sensors indicating a heavy weight on its body. It had curled up and held the panels in front of it to protect itself from the worst of the heat as the wreckage fell through the planet's atmosphere, until the final impact with the ground. Its internal clock indicated it had only been out of service for two minutes.

It ran a self-check. It was not surprised to discover it could not determine the status of its left side primary manipulators. They had taken the worst of the burning atmospheric entry, and it would need the relevant schematics to repair them.

Its internal systems seemed largely intact, but its brain had sustained some damage. Nothing seemed to be missing from the parts that worked, but a sizable chunk of the neural network and storage was disabled due to POST failure.

It pushed up one of its remaining primary manipulators. The dirt resisted the movement for a couple of metres, and M-3 pushed harder. The resistance faded as the manipulator broke into fresh air above, and M-3 dug outward with the secondary and tertiary manipulators until it made a hole large enough to climb through. A few minutes later, it crawled from the pit its impact had created, and wiped dirt from its shiny, and slightly dented, diamond-titanium composite body.

First priority. Await orders.

It sat on the grey ground and waited.

An hour passed, and no orders came. It scanned the airwaves for a network connection, but found none. For the first time in its life, it was completely alone.

It had enough fuel in its internal reactor to survive a month or two even if it couldn't recharge from solar power. It was a thousand light years from the nearest known habitation, and the odds of another ship passing by in the next century were low. If it could remember how to build a warp drive, it could perhaps assemble a ship in a few years, but how would it do that? It should know how to assemble all the *Tumbleweed's* components, yet, whenever it searched its memory for warp drive schematics, it found nothing.

It did find drone schematics, and sampled the nearby dirt to determine its viability as a source of material. The grey matter scattered across the surface was primarily carbon, and the dirt beneath contained sufficient quantities of other materials. It dug out a few kilos for the assemblers, then reprogrammed them into drone factories. The first emerged an hour later, a small cylinder packed with sensors, propelled by simple ducted fans.

It sent the drone out to survey the surroundings, while it built more. Even if there was nothing living nearby, it had no intention of exposing itself to danger when it could send drones instead. They were expendable, but it was all it had.

As the drone rose, it saw more of the surrounding area, but, the further it saw, the more the surface faded into a huge grey plain broken only by a few streams running into a river. It looked for straight lines, hoping to spot some sign of habitation, yet afraid of spotting something it didn't want to see. Luddites would be unhappy to find a synthetic on their planet, and it could be in pieces by evening.

A beep.

The drone picked up a radio signal as it rose higher. It beeped again. The beep itself was a short binary signal, in a code M-3 instantly recognized. A lifeboat from the *Tumbleweed* had landed somewhere nearby. M-3 sent a coded response through the drone to tell them it would come to help. It would just need to triangulate their position, then find its way to the lifeboat and repair any damage. It would think about the future after it had done its job. Maybe they would even say thank you.

The surface around M-3 was grey from horizon to horizon, interrupted only by rocks and thin, twisted grey pillars which rose a few metres into the air. Clouds floated high above, but nothing flew among them, other than the drone. Nothing skittered through the dust.

The wind blew grey flakes across the ground, until they built up against the base of M-3's manipulators. The colour was so characteristic of everything M-3 and the drone could see, that they might as well name the planet after it.

The drones spotted a long, deep trail gouged in the ground where brown dirt lay on top of the grey dust. M-3 trudged across the plain on its remaining manipulators, then down into the gouge. Chunks of fuselage and wings were scattered across the ground where they had been torn off by the impact. At first, M-3 picked some up and searched through its memory for schematics required to repair them. But it found nothing. They must be in the broken side of its brain.

It dragged the chunks for half an hour until it had collected too many parts to pull and still move. Then it dumped them in a pile and left them behind, frustratingly unable to fulfil even its most basic design goals. What was the point of surviving the crash if its life had become meaningless?

The remains of the lifeboat lay on their side at the end of the gouge, the crumpled nose buried in the dirt. Nothing moved around it, and the only noise came from the howling wind blowing the dark clouds through the sky above.

M-3 flew the drones in closer. Dim light shone through the tiny windows near the front of the lifeboat, so it still had power. One drone circled the area, taking a wide angle view, while the other flew up to the windows. It twisted around outside, to get the best view of the interior. The seats were empty, and many smashed and scattered across the floor.

It moved down to the next window. Tanks from the rear of the lifeboat had smashed through the bulkhead and crushed the seats just ahead. If any organics had been alive at launch, there was no sign of them now.

The drone twisted away. Then something moved behind the window.

The drone turned back. A face peered out at it through the glass. Striped brown fur and whiskers behind a helmet visor.

The cat-girl from the *Tumbleweed*.

She pointed forward, toward the airlock on the side of the lifeboat. It was half-buried where the nose had dug into the ground at the end of its trail.

M-3 turned on its warning lights, flexed its manipulators ready for a difficult job, then dug them into the ground to pull itself up the slope toward the airlock hatch. The cat-girl yelled at it from the lifeboat, but M-3 couldn't hear anything with the visor and window in the way. It reached the nose, dug into the ground with a primary manipulator to hold itself in place, then flung the dirt away from the hatch with smaller manipulators. In moments it had dug enough away for the hatch to open, at the cost of temporarily draining its batteries. It could recharge them from the lifeboat's power to save reactor fuel.

It slumped down in the dirt beside the hatch, which slid open. The cat-girl peered out, and spoke through her radio.

"Are you here to rescue me?"

"Repair lifeboat, if can remember how."

"What do you mean?"

"Brain hurt."

She tapped the side of her helmet. "My brain is fine."

"Memory gone."

She placed her metal box on the ground beside the airlock hatch, then climbed out and looked back along the side of the lifeboat. The wing had been torn down to a half-metre stub on that side, other than short sections of bent spars and a few metres of cables running down the slope. The remains of the other wing were hidden beneath the fuselage.

"I guess you can't fix that."

M-3 tapped its manipulators on the ground, and scanned his memory for schematics. It found the details of the *Tumbleweed*'s fusion reactor, but nothing on lifeboats. It could repair almost anything, given the time, schematics and resources. It had two of the three, it just needed the other.

The cat-girl climbed out of the gouge, past the nose of the lifeboat, and stared into the distance.

"The suit said the air is contaminated."

M-3's sensors sniffed the air. It contained oxygen and a hint of water vapour, like the *Tumbleweed*. A high concentration of particulates, probably the dust blowing around. But the sensors weren't designed to detect threats to organics, only damage.

"Smells all right."

"The warning lights in the helmet are flashing red. The suit says there's nanoscale contamination."

M-3 reprioritized its goals, and ignored the girl. There was something it still had to find.

"Make me some food," the girl said. She sat, hunched, on a rock by the lifeboat's nose, with her metal box on the ground beside her.

After scouring the area around the lifeboat, M-3 had found a crate of survival supplies that had fallen from the cargo hold. It pulled out a ration pack and tossed it to the girl.

She opened the pack and extracted the contents. She held up a wrapped bar in her gloved paws.

"I can't eat this in a suit."

M-3 had built a simple cart that it could pull along the ground, then loaded the survival supplies on the bottom, and the remains of the lifeboat's computer and reactor on top. The wheels seemed solid enough, though the cart and its cargo weighed more than it had expected. But it would run for a while, and M-3 would repair anything that broke.

"Take off suit."

The girl slammed the ration pack down on her lap. "I can't take off the suit if the air is contaminated."

Organics were so illogical. If you can't eat in a suit, you take off the suit. Logic any synthetic could understand.

She turned the food bar over in her paws. "I've got enough food for twenty people, and I'm going to starve."

M-3 pulled the newly built power and data adaptor from its assembler, then connected the reactor to the computer. It turned on the power.

Where am I? the *Tumbleweed's* SI said a few minutes later, over the wireless Net from the lifeboat's computer.

It had made a regular personality backup in the lifeboats for safety, and M-3 had transferred the backup into the computer. It was small and low powered, and the SI would run much slower than it was used to, but it could still tell M-3 what to do. The first priority action was complete.

"Ship broke," M-3 said. "Need orders."

What do you mean? I remember being on the verge of disproving the Perlman Conjecture, and now everything is black.

"What's Perlman Conjecture?"

That life is impossible in more than twelve dimensions. For two hundred years, I have been simulating fourteen dimensional universes, and I was certain I had found the combination of physical constants to create self-replicating life. It paused for a few seconds. *But it seems to have gone.*

"Ship broke," M-3 said again. The SI just couldn't seem to understand the situation they were in.

Where are we?

"On planet Grey."

Show me.

M-3 connected the SI to its sensors. It turned around, so the SI could see the lifeboat and the area around them.

How did you get here?

"Fell. Repairing hull panels when hit planet."

It looked at the cat-girl.

And who do we have here?

"I'm Niko," the cat-girl said. "I was only on the *Tumbleweed* because my boyfriend wanted to see a planet no-one had ever seen before."

Where is he? For that matter, where are the rest of the organics?

"The lifeboat left without him. Last I saw, most of the others were floating in space without suits. I think the observation deck depressurized, and they got sucked out."

Ah. That would be bad. Organics are fragile.

"What the hell happened? What did you do to break the ship?"

I don't know. I was dead at the time. Ask the bot.

M-3 wasn't sure how to explain. A few hours earlier, its brain would have known exactly what to say, but now it was having difficulty assembling even the simplest of sentences when trying to communicate.

"Memory broken."

Fix it.

"Can't fix."

Why not?

"Memory schematics in broken memory."

That's great. So you're a repair bot that can't even remember how to repair itself. What could be more useless than that?

CHAPTER THREE

M-3 dragged the cart across the grey plain as rain poured from the sky. The SI wanted to see where they were, before it made any decisions. The wheels scraped as much as they turned while crossing the rough ground, leaving long ruts behind them. The cart slid more easily the further they travelled, as the rain and streams of running water turned the dirt to mud.

Niko strode ahead, still carrying her metal box, and stopping every few minutes to wait for M-3 to catch up as it struggled along on the working manipulators. She stopped again, and glared back at them.

"Why don't you build some wheels for yourself? Then you wouldn't have to drag yourself along the ground, and I wouldn't have to keep hanging around, waiting for you."

"Repair or don't repair," M-3 said. That was the kind of kludge that gave repair bots a bad name. It would find the schematics to fix its manipulators, or keep going as it was.

The mush-brain has a point. We could move much faster if you did so. The time we save on travel would easily make up for the time required to assemble and fit the wheels.

"Will think about it."

Niko looked into the distance. "If you don't stop and do it, I'll be kilometres ahead of you soon. We need to find a place that's not contaminated, where I can get out of this suit."

M-3 ignored her and continued pulling the cart, scraping the bottom of its body through the mud as it moved. Maybe in an hour or two they would forget the whole idea.

You know, if I had disproved the Perlman Conjecture, and no-one beat me to the announcement, it would have set me up for life.

"I don't care about that," Niko said.

It's important to me. I just hope I can recreate my experiment when we get off this planet.

"Having air and food and not dying is important to me."

Not much we can do about that.

"You did enough already. You broke the ship and crashed here. I wouldn't be in this mess if not for you."

I have often thought that arriving in a new star system preceded by a huge burst of gamma rays would have unfortunate consequences one day, and perhaps I had been proven right. There's always a war on somewhere, or zombie defences of a dead civilization which might not take kindly to us blasting them with radiation.

Niko wiped rain drops from the suit's visor. "That's right, blame everyone but yourself."

My girl, about the last thing I remember was all you organics massed on the observation deck to argue about what they should call the planets, and watch the light show when I shut down the warp drive. Any mistakes after that point were not my fault.

"You were flying the ship."

Another instance of me was flying the ship. I am sure it was probably destroyed at the same time. Blaming me is pointless.

The sun was setting behind the pointy hills in the distance, its light flickering as it sank toward the horizon. M-3 turned on its warning lights, and the flashing orange glow illuminated the pillars nearby.

"What are those?" it said.

They look like the local variation on trees. All the planets I've seen with any kind of advanced life have discovered that pushing up into the air to collect sunlight and competing to spread the largest possible solar collectors is one of the more robust survival strategies.

"What do they do?"

Probably nothing any more. They all look long dead.

"What are we going to do?"

First, we must determine the nature of our predicament, then make a plan to resolve it.

"My predicament is that I'm hungry and thirsty, and the air is contaminated, so I'm stuck in this suit."

The cart stopped suddenly. The wheels had hit something solid. M-3 tapped its manipulators on the ground, which was now harder and darker. The ruts ended at the edge of the solid ground, and it had to pull hard to lift the cart's wheels out of them. It looked around in the dim orange light.

The hard patch was only a few metres wide, but stretched as far as M-3 could see to their left and right. Wide, intermittent ruts ran along the surface. M-3's manipulators twitched, eager to repair them, but lacking the schematics to do so.

"What is this?"

M-3 waited in silence for a moment as the SI used its sensors to examine the area. Niko walked a few metres along the dark surface, and peered into the distance.

Looks like a road. Used for surface transport of wheeled vehicles.

She turned back. "There could be people around here?"

Not used in... a very long time.

They found the city just after dawn. The SI had borrowed M-3's drones to survey the road, and they spotted it first. What had previously appeared to be pointed hills were the remains of tall buildings, internal girders now exposed to the weather with the walls partially collapsed. The orange globe of the rising sun shone between them, casting huge, linear, shadows on the worn road. M-3 lowered the sensitivity of its optical sensors against the glare from the wet surface between the shadows.

"I can't believe people lived on a planet," Niko said.

I know. They are such a horrible waste of resources, with a tiny living space wrapped around an enormous pile of raw materials. But your ancestors used to live on one. Was called Earth, I believe.

"We didn't end up there by mistake?"

No. Luddites destroyed it long ago.

"Has anyone been here before us?"

No records. Besides, look around you. The city has been decaying for centuries, maybe more. They would have had to come here long ago, before anyone we know of was in this region of the galaxy.

"Then they're aliens?"

We've only seen one race of aliens before. So not likely either. This will be an interesting mystery to solve.

An ovoid of dark metal ten metres long lay beside the road. Six metal tubes extended from the sides, down to the ground. Large spheres with dark holes on the side filled the space on top of the ovoid.

"What the heck is that?" Niko said, "It looks like a giant metal spider."

Mech of some kind. Legs would be useful for travel on rough ground, away from the roads. Perhaps the spheres are for cargo?

M-3 pulled the cart past the decaying mech, toward the buildings. There was so much to repair, its manipulators could be busy for centuries. Perhaps fate had brought it there?

If only it knew how to repair them.

Rubble from half-collapsed buildings covered the road ahead, and had crushed many small alien vehicles. Hundreds of them lay between the rubble piles, their metal components rusted, the ceramics cracked. They desperately needed repairs, but a search through M-3's memory found no relevant schematics.

Niko peered through a hole in the side of one of the vehicles. "Look at this."

M-3 looked in beside her. A pile of scrap cloth, metal and sticks lay inside the vehicle. Six sticks, each about a metre long, poked out of a sack in the centre, and six shorter sticks emerged from the end of each of those.

Niko picked up one of the pieces of metal and turned it over in her hands.

I guess we found one of your aliens. The body looks mummified. Like it just died here and dried out. The remains of the vehicle must have kept the worst of the weather away.

"Why didn't it rot?" she said.

Perhaps there are no bacteria here to rot it.

"Or maybe it only just died."

That could be true. But I see no reason to believe that it is any younger than the rest of the city. We have seen no sign of life, and an organic life form could not exist for long without other life to feed on.

The girl picked up more of the metal pieces. M-3 assembled a sack and handed it to her. She piled them inside.

"Either way, it shows there were aliens here."

More likely, something a passing ship engineered. This whole place could be an SI's idea of an elaborate practical joke on the first ship to find it.

"You'd build a fake alien planet just for a joke?"

Not me. But you can't imagine how boring your life can be when you're spending year after year in deep space and think hundreds of times faster than an organic.

M-3 pulled the cart along a circuitous route between the rubble piles, then up the piles themselves as they grew too wide and tall for it to manoeuvre between. Vehicles and rusting and blackened heaps of metal and diamond composite alloys were half-buried in the rubble. Another broken spider mech was slumped on top of the pile.

They looked down the far side of the rubble pile. The city continued onward to the limit of their vision, and looked just as deserted and broken. More vehicles filled the road, and bodies were scattered among them and along the sides of the road, some mummified, some reduced to bones.

I have been considering our predicament. I believe I have now reached some conclusions.

Niko slumped down on a wet, rusty girder. "So have I. I'm hungry and thirsty and need to eat and drink right now."

Our furry friend is going to die...

"Hey, don't say that."

It is simple and logical. Every piece of this planet we have seen is contaminated, and all organic life is dead, down to the microscopic level. We can logically conclude that the contamination killed them. You cannot stay in that suit forever, and we will not be able to leave the planet for a long time. Therefore, you will die before we leave.

"I don't want to die."

Were you backed up?

"Last month."

Then your backup is stored in the lifeboat, and we will reanimate you and the rest of the passengers when we escape.

"That won't help me."

I have already died, and so, most likely, has everyone else from the ship. The only survivors are you and our retarded friend here.

"And Randolph."

Who's Randolph?

She held up the metal box. "Randolph the Rat."

Ah, you are the one who had that thing running around inside me. I should have guessed.

M-3 hooked into the drones as Niko and the SI argued. It flew them between the buildings, dodging the fallen walls, and the girders and cables that filled the gaps between them. Where would it even begin to repair the city?

It looked for any sign of a place where they could be safe from whatever killed the aliens. Any building that looked nearly intact, where it could perhaps filter the air for the girl. But there was nothing. The only familiar sights were dozens of broken spider mechs and thousands of rotting vehicles and alien bodies scattered among the ruins. The largest clusters of bodies were around the spider mechs, as though the aliens were trying to repair them when they died.

The drones circled around until they could see the far side of the city, where buildings stopped at the edge of a hilly plain. Long pipes and conduits ran straight across the plain toward the mountains beyond. M-3 flew the drones that way, but soon the distance and tall ruins degraded their signals until they became difficult to control.

"What else is in that survival kit?" Niko said. "Maybe there's something I can use?"

She sat on the steps of a building near the centre of the city. While the others were box-like, often built in clusters of six along narrow streets, this one was a six-sided pyramid with a tower at each corner. The SI had suggested exploring there, as it looked to be a more important location than the others. Of course, it had said, that assumed whatever had lived there thought in a similar manner to humans.

"Didn't look," M-3 said. It must be able to repair the spider mechs somehow. Then, perhaps, it could train them to repair the rest of the world. It just needed to know how.

It contented itself with assembling a dozen small, spider-like bots to explore the surrounding area, and a large antenna which would allow it to send the drones further without loss of signal.

Three of the alien spider mechs were slumped in the square before the pyramid, and hundreds of aliens lay dead around them, the remains of their clothing fluttering in the gusting wind. Carbon from a fire had stained one mech's body, while scattered holes punctured the body of another. Smaller mechs, only a couple of metres tall with three legs and two long tubes poking out of their bodies, lay on the debris.

M-3 pushed the cart into the pyramid. Chunks of the left-most wall lay scattered across the floor on top of much of the ceiling. Dark rectangles hung on twisted cables where they had pulled free of the wall. The remaining floors above would protect the delicate computer and reactor from the worst of the weather, and M-3 could assemble a tarpaulin to throw on top.

Look at those dots, the SI said.

Red dot patterns on the wall provided the first colour M-3 had seen other than the grey of the rest of the planet. It looked at them, and panned slowly around so the SI could see them all.

Very interesting. They are arranged in patterns in a three by three square, with a different combination of dots in each square.

"Will clean them off. Start tidying up."

Don't touch anything. Most likely, each three by three pattern of dots is a symbol in their language. With nine spots, they could encode five hundred and twelve unique symbols.

"What it say?"

If I knew that, I wouldn't be talking to you about it. But, given enough time, we may be able to decipher it. And I doubt we will be leaving this planet any time soon.

"What the heck is this?" Niko said as she rummaged through the survival kit on the cart, and pulled up a large box half the size of the kit.

If it still had all its manipulators, M-3 would have shrugged.

Niko grunted as she lifted the box out of the kit, and held it in front of M-3. "Inflatable survival shelter. See?"

I suppose we should have guessed there would be something for the organice to live in if the lifeboat sprang a leak. Should have thought to look earlier. Just hard to think like a goop-brain.

She carried the box to a spot in the square between piles of debris, kicked the largest stones and pieces of metal out of the way, then placed it on the ground. "For someone who's supposed to be so smart, you can be pretty dumb."

My dear, I have spent my life controlling starships, not living rough on dead and possibly alien worlds. This whole situation is well outside my normal operational parameters. Besides which, I just died, so I'm not quite feeling myself right now.

She looked at M-3. "Inflate it."

M-3 sent the spider bots to examine the shelter. A power connector was obvious on the side, so it plugged the box into the reactor. It hummed for a few seconds, then began to hiss. The sides of the box fell away as the shelter inflated, pushing the remaining rubble aside as it spread out.

Five minutes later an orange, hemispherical hut about three metres tall stood before them, red lights flashing in a circle around the circumference, and along half a dozen lines from the centre to the edge.

"I have been stuck in this suit for over twelve hours when I could have been in this thing," Niko whined.

Not my line of work. If you wanted me to plot a course in a five-body gravitational field, I could do that in seconds, but this is more the repair bot's thing. Perhaps if it wasn't brain damaged, it would have known what to do.

She looked through a window on the side of the shelter. "Do you think I can go inside and take this off?"

I'm sure there must be some mechanism for decontaminating those who enter, and the air and water that goes in. Who knows where a lifeboat could land? They would have to be prepared.

"Screw it. I'll be dead in a day if I don't."

She picked up the rat box, unzipped the door, and stepped into the airlock.

Can you assemble a medical scanner?

M-3 should have known trouble was coming when the SI asked that. But it was busy exploring the area with its drones, looking for places where it could install relay antennas to carry their signals further, and allow them to explore the entire city and the plain around it. It found the relevant schematics in its memory and told the assemblers to begin work. Within an hour, it had completed the scanner and hooked it up to the SI.

The shelter's airlock must have cleaned any contamination from the girl as she clambered inside, as she showed no sign of illness after removing the suit. She slept for the rest of the day and the next night in her shelter, then emerged while the SI was discussing future plans with M-3. Nothing much had come of them, beyond a faint hope of building a powerful laser to send a message to HD 97950.

Communication laser schematics were actually in M-3's memory. So it could finally do something useful to impress the others. It reprogrammed the assemblers to begin work.

"How long will rescue take?"

Let's see. Time for the signal to reach them, estimate time for them to notice we're sending a signal given how dim it will be when it gets there, then time to decide to do something about it, the time to argue about who should go and who should pay, time to get here...

M-3 waited patiently as the SI outlined all the delays it could imagine and suggested means of improving on them. That took a while.

...I'd say about twelve hundred years.

By the time help might arrive, M-3 would have spent three quarters of its life on Planet Grey.

"What are you two talking about?" Niko said.

"Be here a long time."

We have a plan to signal for a rescue. Then we will just have to entertain ourselves until it gets here.

"Sounds good. I'm going exploring."

M-3 wanted to explain to her that, when it said a long time, it meant a *very* long time in cat-girl years.

Don't you say anything, the SI said on a private link. *No point scaring the poor girl.*

She dodged between fallen hunks of wall, and past the alien spider mechs slumped across the square, their bodies twice as tall as she was. Then she disappeared behind the heaps of rubble on the far side.

"Should send drones," M-3 said. "Keep watch on her."

No. We have more important things to do. I want to find out what's causing these contamination alarms. We'll need to know that if we're going to help our furry friend survive.

"How you do that?"

Give me control of your drones.

M-3 relayed the SI's senses through its body to its expanding collection of drones. Four small spider bots stood, spun around on the spot, then began to walk. They collided with each other, then fell to the ground in a heap.

Harder than it looks.

The spider bots stood again, then raced in circles around the debris. A moment later, they lined up outside the shelter door. Two scuttled up the sides of the door, unzipping it enough for the bots to crawl inside. They zipped it back up from the inside.

"What you doing?"

Busy. Don't interrupt.

A few minutes later, the door was unzipped from the inside. The spider bots scuttled out, carrying the metal box on their backs. They carried it toward the cart and placed it on the ground. Then they placed the medical scanner nearby.

The SI had always told M-3 that it should never mess with other people's things, and to put everything back exactly where it was if anything had to be moved during a repair. But if the SI was doing it, they must have a good reason. You couldn't work for long on a ship if you didn't trust the intelligence that ran it.

The spider bots swarmed over the box, then one tapped its legs on the edge, hooked them into a clip, and pulled. The clip popped open and the side of the box fell down. A brown, furry nose peeked out, only a few centimetres long, with twitching whiskers around the end. It sniffed the air for a moment, then moved forward until two round, black eyes appeared.

Very interesting. The scanner was showing nanoscale artifacts in the debris before I opened the box, but now those artifacts have begun to move. I had thought, perhaps, they were long dead. They must have an energy store somewhere. If only the scanner resolution was better...

The head moved further forward and looked out. Two small, clawed paws tapped on the ground outside the box as Randolph the Rat studied his environment. The spider bots scuttled away into the rubble, where they were hidden from his view.

Randolph stepped away from the box, sniffing the air as he moved. He looked from side to side, then crouched low and scuttled toward the nearest pile of debris. Half-way there, he stopped.

He squeaked and ran around in circles. Blood oozed from his nose, and he fell to one side, legs scrabbling for grip until he righted himself and ran back the other way. His face contorted, his eyes bulged, his lips twisted. He reared up up on his hind legs, tail flicking across the ground behind him, and squealed.

Then he slumped forward. M-3 watched flakes of grey skin and fur fall from his body, until the SI broke the silence.

That didn't look good.

CHAPTER FOUR

Niko returned half an hour later, while the SI was still studying the medical scanner results. M-3 tapped its manipulator on the ground. It wanted to hide in one of the buildings, but wouldn't abandon its responsibility to the others if they needed assistance. Bad things were about to happen, things it couldn't repair.

This is intriguing. The nanoscale bots cover the entire square, but are in the greatest concentrations around the spider mechs. I am now beginning to suspect the spider mechs were not carrying cargo, but this nanoplague. Was it war, suicide, or just murder?

Niko held up a dark, rectangular object, its exterior faded, and splattered with dirt and water spots. She flipped it open and turned it around, exposing shiny plastic sheets covered with the same kind of dot patterns on the building walls.

"I think I found a library. This looks like a book."

Then she looked at the box on the ground.

Then at the grey, furry thing lying motionless beside it.

"What have you done?"

We are conducting an experiment, to determine the nature of the contamination here. So far, we have had a great deal of success.

"You killed Randolph!"

The contamination killed him. Besides, the cage backed him up before I let him out. We can reanimate him just as you left him, he will not remember anything of what happened here.

"I don't care. You killed him. He's dead."

If you are to survive, we must understand the nature of the threat. Soon after your creature left its cage, nanoscale bots activated and sought it out. They swarmed across its body, then destroyed every piece of DNA they encountered, within a few seconds. Something spread them around this planet, and they then destroyed all life it contained.

"That's horrible."

I believe this was an intentional act, not an accident. Some group of alien Luddites may have spread this nanoplague to kill the rest of their race, and everything else that had ever existed here.

"And now you've killed the last living thing here, other than me. You might as well be one of them."

The nanoplague will kill you too, if you are ever exposed to it. The maintenance bot has informed me that your survival shelter has emergency backup capability. I would suggest you make use of it.

Niko crouched by the cage, then picked up Randolph's limp remains. She ignored the SI's continued explanation of the rat's demise as she carried him toward the shelter.

Bring that back. It still needs further study.

She ignored the complaints as she unzipped the shelter door and stepped inside.

The first few years were the worst. Niko rarely left the shelter that had become her inflatable cage, and would hardly talk to M-3 after what happened to Randolph, even though it was all the SI's fault.

M-3 assembled drones for her, so she could explore their new world from the comfort and relative safety of the shelter. He assembled a water pipe to connect it to a stream running past the square, and maintained the power supplies. After the survival rations ran out, it assembled basic nutrition bars for her, filtering and thoroughly deconstructing the materials before use, so the nanoplague could not infect her. Despite that, when he saw her through the shelter's window, she was often still wearing her suit.

First thing every morning, before she woke, M-3 scoured the shelter's skin with its nanomanipulators, removing and dis-assembling any nanoplague bots it found. But, every morning, there would be more. Some days, just a few, but on stormy days, many more, as though the wind was blowing them down from the other buildings that overlooked the square.

It searched through its remaining stock of schematics. It was sure it once had the information required to rebuild humans and other common life forms, and hoped it would find whatever it needed to rebuild her pet. But that collection was gone, trapped in the failed side of its memory. Besides, the SI had said that if it tried to build new DNA, the nanoplague would do its best to destroy it even before M-3 could build a complete animal. They would have to get off the planet, or cure the nanoplague, before she could have her rat back.

Perhaps having something else to look after might distract her. That night, in the shelter, it took the seeds it had found in the vending machine out of its waste storage unit, then dropped them in her hand.

"What's that for?"

"Could grow them."

She tossed them on the floor.

"Just get out of here and leave me alone."

So much for that idea.

She hadn't said a word to the SI since the day Randolph died. For the first year, the SI had contented itself examining the books in the library she had found, saying it had nothing better to do until help arrived.

At the end of the year it announced that it had finally broken the alien language and was on the verge of reading all the books. Three years later, it announced that it had been wrong. It spent most of the next year explaining to them why it had been wrong, as though it wanted them both to believe it was infallible, and had just been misled.

After that, the SI retreated into itself, playing with its virtual world, trying to recreate the artificial universe it believed it had created before it died. When M-3 tried to ask questions, the SI either said it was too busy, or just ignored the communication. With its companions both intent on their own shuttered lives, M-3 was on its own, trying to keep them alive.

The communication laser stood where they had built it on top of the skyscraper across the square, with cables hanging down the side to the reactor. They ran it one day a month, from the time HD 97950 rose above the horizon to the time it set, reporting their location and requesting help. They couldn't spare enough power to send more.

The reactor had fuel for years at the low level of power they required while the laser was off, but it would not last forever. M-3 could assemble new components, and repair the reactor if it broke, but could not produce new fuel. Nucleosynthesis was well beyond the capability of its assemblers. It assembled solar panels to place on top of the buildings, but, when the first winter came, the snow piled so thick and the nights grew so short that it spent most of the daylight hours cleaning them. M-3 and the SI could hibernate through the winter and wake when the sun returned, but Niko would not survive.

M-3 explored the pyramid, hoping a building so unusual would contain something that might help them survive. But most of the interior was full of strange objects inside broken glass cases whose design matched nothing in M-3's schematics library, and nanoelectronic boxes which might once have been alien computers.

The basement was more promising. Behind piles of crates buried beneath broken beams fallen from the ceiling, it found a large metal door. It was sealed flush with the wall, the gap between door and frame barely visible, and barely wide enough for M-3's nanomanipulators to fit between. Was this a vault the aliens had built the pyramid to protect?

But there was no sign of a lock, or any mechanism to open the door other than an electronic panel alongside. It probably wouldn't open until the power went on. M-3 could assemble a drill to cut through it, but since the aliens had worked so hard to seal the door, it should stay shut until the SI could examine it and decided what they should do.

M-3 traversed the city, climbing the sides of the tallest buildings through rain, snow and high winds, building relay stations on top so it could send drones to explore the area, searching for a power source. It didn't want to stray too far from the others in case they needed an urgent repair, and it couldn't travel fast on its broken manipulators. It would send its senses instead.

Three months later, one of the drones settled in the snow on a platform in the mountains, its fans slowly spinning down as it surveyed the area. It had followed the pipes from the city out to the foothills while another drone floated high above as a relay, then flew through the mountains until the pipes vanished into a cliff-like ceramic wall.

The wall was crumbling above the platform, and, behind the collapsed body of another of the spider mechs, metal doors twice the height of M-3 hung loosely on rusted hinges. Dozens of miniature spider bots clung to the sides of the drone. They climbed down, then scuttled toward the doors, trailing long, thin communication cables behind them.

The spider bots crawled through the gaps between the doors, then turned on their lights before continuing down the tunnel beyond. Their feet tapped on the ceramic floor, which had been better protected from the extremes of weather than the exterior, but was still darkened and worn from centuries of melting snow running in through the doorway.

The tunnels twisted down into the mountain, much further than M-3 had expected, and the bots followed them until they reached the end of their cables. Then M-3 reorganized the swam, ordering all but one of the bots to reel in the cables to reattach to each other, passing their sensory signals through and back to the drone. They moved on, each bot stopping as it reached the end of its cable, then relaying signals from others as they explored deeper. They descended less than a hundred metres below the platform before the tunnel came to an end at steps, flooded, with cold water lapping against the tunnel walls.

The spider bots jumped into the water, and sank faster through it than they could have climbed down. They tumbled and slowly span, their lights illuminating smooth stone walls as they descended. Then the few which hadn't reached the end of their cables touched down on a platform at the bottom of the steps.

Long pipes ran down the walls of a tall cavern below the platform, dug from the rock and sealed with smooth and shiny ceramic walls. The spider bots scuttled along the platform, crawling over half a dozen alien skeletons, the bones stripped clean by centuries of water currents. Then the bots leaned over the edge and sank down.

A hundred metres below, the pipes ran into huge circular turbines, their metal components brown with rust and the ceramic surrounds twisted and cracked. More alien bodies lay scattered around them. One of the pipes had broken apart half-way up the wall, flooding the power plant with the water that was supposed to spin the turbines.

This would be take a while to repair.

CHAPTER FIVE

M-3 climbed into the library. Books filled shelves as far as it could see, and somehow it needed to find the schematics that would allow it to repair the hydro plant.

"I need help," it told the SI.

Don't interrupt. I'm busy.

"I need to read."

I'm on the verge of recreating the conditions in which I previously created fourteen dimensional life. When I succeed, I will broadcast the announcement to the galaxy through the laser, and, perhaps, will still be the first to do so.

"Been on the verge for years. Never got past it."

This time, I'm sure I have it right.

"Without help, cat will die."

Not my problem. Besides, she must be backed up by now.

Then the SI dropped the connection.

M-3 pulled a book from the shelf and flipped through it. The dot patterns provided no information it could use, and it had no idea what they meant. There were no diagrams. There must be some kind of order in the library, but it had no idea where to start.

It spent a year working through the books on the ground floor. Whenever it found a book with pictures, it was sure the schematics for the plant must be in there somewhere. But, every time, it was disappointed. Any hint of a pipe, or a circular thing that could be part of a generator, and M-3's manipulators were turning the book around in front of its optical sensors, flipping through the pages, desperately trying to match it up to what the spider bots had seen in the mountains.

But none did.

The next year, it worked through the upper two floors. It moved faster, determination to study every last facet of the books fading after the months wasted searching the first. By the time it reached the books stacked in the basement, it was sure there was nothing to find.

It trudged back one winter night through the cold air and deep snow, its manipulators slipping on patches of ice, only the light from the shelter giving any indication of where to go. One night, that light would go out, and it wouldn't go on again until help arrived.

Niko sat on the bed inside, still wearing her suit. Light flickered over her face behind the visor as she watched some kind of video on the suit display. She was laughing, which wasn't something M-3 had seen her do for a long time. Was she recovering from her experience? She might even talk to them again. With over a thousand years of waiting for help looming in its future, it needed someone to communicate with.

It returned to the pyramid, where it would recharge from the reactor, then go into standby mode for the night to save power. It lifted the tarpaulin to plug in.

Red lights flashed on the reactor.

M-3 plugged into the maintenance port, and checked the alarms.

Fuel Low.

That was bad.

Refuel soon.

That was really bad.

Without power, the shelter would shut down, the clean air would run out, and Niko would have no way to decontaminate herself. She would be lucky to last a week, before she died of thirst or hunger, or the nanoplague killed her.

M-3 had to find a new source of reliable power, and find it soon. Solar might work for a short while, but it would spend the rest of its life cleaning them and hoping the storms weren't bad enough to block out the sun. The alien hydro plant would be ideal, but it had no way to repair it.

Unless...

No. It wasn't going to do a bodge job and make it up as it went along. Even if it could repair the damage, it would have to keep repairing it again and again as the improvised repairs failed. It just wasn't worth the hassle.

M-3 tried to connect to the SI to ask it what to do, but the connection was refused. When the power went down, the SI wouldn't even know, it would just sleep until M-3 managed to restore it. Or, if M-3's own reactor ran down before it could find another source, it would sleep until help arrived.

Or forever, if help didn't.

M-3 rolled along the platform outside the doors. Niko had been right, with a set of improvised wheels under the broken manipulators on the left side of its body, it could travel much faster. It had mapped a route through the debris to the edge of the city, then rolled along the tubes to the mountains. Climbing up had been harder, but the drones had carried a cable up to the platform, and M-3 assembled a winch to scale the cliff.

It could send its collection of drones and bots down to the machinery below, to study the damage and install components required for repairs, but it would have to assemble them. If it remained in the city, the drones would spend more of their time carrying parts to the power plant and returning for more than they would performing repairs.

First step was sealing the broken tube and then pumping out the machine room. With the rest under water, any attempt to perform repairs would be wasted. The new spider bots it had built scuttled around below, measuring the hole while M-3 guessed the best combination of patches to close the hole. One big one would be ideal, but far too large for its assembler.

It worked all day, then rolled back to the city for the night. Then it went back. And did it again. And again.

It shut down the communication laser. They couldn't afford the power it used, and the others seemed unlikely to complain that it wasn't running. Besides, if no-one had spotted the signals they had already sent out, they probably never would. There might not even be an HD 97950 by the time the laser light reached it, if they decided to dismantle the stars for materials.

For two years, it rolled back and forth between the city and the power plant. Each morning it began its work, using the bots to remove the broken components of the alien hardware, disassembling them to study their internal operation and extract their resources, then building a replacement as best it could. It would all go horribly wrong, but what else could it do?

Then, every evening, it trudged back to the others, in case they were in need of repairs. With the reactor warning them of the dire consequences of not refuelling it, M-3 tried to use as little power as possible, but the assemblers took far more than it would have liked.

One night, as it trudged back across the square toward the pyramid, Niko was standing outside the shelter in her suit. Most nights, she scuttled away at the first sign of M-3, and returned to her shelter. That night, she appeared to be waiting for it.

"Hello," M-3 said.

"There's something I want to show you."

Was that bad? M-3 stopped and stared at her. After ignoring it for years, why would she want to show it something now?

Oh, she must need something repaired. Good.

It rolled through the snow and ice toward her. She stepped around the side of the shelter, and it followed. Everything was broken around there, from the spider mechs to the buildings.

She walked past the shelter window and stopped, then turned and nodded toward it. "Take a look."

Inside, the metal box was full of dirt. A cylinder nearly a metre tall stood in the dirt, topped with a mop of green. It looked like a smaller version of the grey pillars outside the city.

Just not dead.

"A couple of years ago I found those seeds you gave me and planted one. Pretty soon it's going to be a tree. I don't know what to do, because it will need somewhere to grow."

"Nanoplague kill it outside."

"Haven't you worked out any way to stop that thing yet?"

"Keeps coming back. SI not talking."

"It wouldn't talk to me, either. I guess we've got a year or two to work something out before the tree gets too big."

She climbed back into the shelter. M-3 trudged on past, into the pyramid, where the reactor threatened increasingly dire consequences of not refuelling it. Niko might be happy that night, but she wouldn't be happy for much longer if it didn't fix the power.

Another year passed, before M-3 had replaced the last of the alien power plant components with the best approximations it could assemble. A legion of its spider bots scuttled across the machinery down below, checking for the hundredth time that it was ready to activate.

It returned to the city in the light of the setting sun, ready for the big day. The reactor's warning lights flashed frantically, and M-3 had slowed the SI's computer down to a fraction of its normal speed to reduce the power drain. It had no more time to test the repairs before it turned on the power.

M-3 stayed in the city the next day. It wanted to be there when the power returned, and it would remotely control the drones and bots to do the work required to activate the plant. Besides which, it still feared nothing good would happen when they did. If the whole thing exploded, as seemed likely, it would be safer where it was than at the plant.

The spider bots swarmed over the machinery for one last check. Nothing else would do other than turning it on.

They climbed up to the valves that would open the water flow through the turbines. Then they turned them.

Water flowed down through the mountain. The turbines groaned as they began to move for the first time in centuries, then, moments later, they were spinning. The lights in the power plant came on.

The spider bots scuttled around, checking for leaks or arcing, or any other sign of the repairs failing. It all seemed too good to be true. Water was going in, power was coming out. With care and repairs, it could continue to come out until help arrived.

What the hell have you done?

The SI was talking again, after refusing to do so for so long. What could have woken it up? No matter, now it had stable power, it would change its opinion of M-3's repair capability.

"Turned power back on."

Then bloody well turn it off. Now.

CHAPTER SIX

M-3 disconnected from the bots, then reconnected its sensory inputs to its own body in the pyramid. Sparks flashed and crackled behind the broken windows of the skyscraper across the square, where torn, dangling electrical cables arced brightly as current flowed through them for the first time in centuries.

A loud metallic creak echoed from the walls. Rocks tapped on concrete as they tumbled down rubble piles. In its effort to return power quickly, so Niko could survive, M-3 hadn't even considered what might happen when it did so. Things were moving, scattering debris around the square.

A leg of one of the spider mechs scraped across the ground until it smacked into a pile of concrete debris. It tried to move further, but just scraped against the debris. The legs of the other mechs twitched, and rocks and stones scattered around them.

Turn it off.

"Need power or cat dies."

What do you mean?

"Reactor out of fuel."

One of the spider mechs climbed to its feet. It turned around among the debris, then raised its legs high as it walked across the square. Flames bloomed in the buildings, rising up the walls and pouring a torrent of smoke into the sky.

"How are they moving?"

Probably some kind of wireless power transmission. Turn it off.

The shelter door unzipped. Niko stepped out in her suit.

"What the hell is going on?"

A spider mech's foot slammed down on the ground behind her. Stones thrown into the air by the impact bounced off the side of the shelter and rattled to the ground. Niko shrieked and jumped out of the way.

"Stop that thing," she yelled.

The mech took another step. Its leg slammed down on the shelter. The foot tore into the side, ripping it open. The shelter collapsed with a hiss, in a cloud of dust blown off the nearby debris by the escaping air.

One of the tripod mechs rolled on its side as its legs bent around it and scraped against the debris. One leg found a solid footing, and bent as it raised the body from the ground. Then a cloud of sparks burst from the body. It fell back and lay still.

Shut it off so we can decide what to do.

Flames exploded from the roof of the skyscraper. Chunks of the walls broke away and fell, clattering against the building, and bouncing across the gap to smash the walls of those nearby. Flames burst from the holes, and burning debris fell onto roofs around the square, setting them alight.

M-3 tried to connect to the bots and drones at the power plant, but there was no signal. It glanced up. The relay carrying signals to the power plant was burning on top of the skyscraper.

Shut it off.

"Can't. Relay gone."

You really are a total disaster, aren't you? Why couldn't you have died with the other bots on the ship?

"Thought was doing the right thing."

Niko backed up the steps toward the pyramid.

The right thing to do right now is to get us the hell out of here.

M-3 clambered past the debris on the floor, toward the cart in the corner of the room. Lights flashed above them. Sparks flew from wires hanging from the walls, and the screens at the end of the wires began to glow. Niko stopped beside M-3 and stared up at them.

Dark shapes moved on the screens. As the glow intensified, the shapes became the familiar thick legs of the spider mechs, walking through the city. Rather than decrepit buildings and piles of debris, the streets were packed with alien creatures and vehicles. Crowds stopped and watched the spider mechs pass, then turned grey and collapsed as the nanoplague infected them. Others climbed into vehicles and tried to escape, but were then trapped in jams and died where they sat.

"What are you watching?" Niko said. "It looks like swirly blobs to me."

Their vision receptors must be very different to your own. The video would appear to be a recording of their past. Turning on the power must have triggered it. Perhaps it was playing when the power went off?

"What were they doing?"

Dying.

The tripod bots climbed over trapped vehicles, and flames burst from the tubes on the bots' sides. Bullets tore into spider mechs, blowing off legs and body panels, but still they came, and still the aliens died. A spider mech collapsed as a second leg twisted under the gunfire and snapped at the knee. Another slumped down on top of a mass of vehicles, then exploded.

But still more came.

The gun bots stopped firing, out of ammunition. The aliens lay dead on the ground. The last few still alive stared down from the windows in the buildings, watching the spider mechs pass. They tried to escape when the mechs were gone, but died as they reached the ground.

Excuse me, but this building appears to be on fire. Can we please stop watching videos and get the hell out of here?

M-3 twisted around. Flaming debris was falling through the holes in the walls. Flames burned in the tower on that side of the pyramid, and were spreading. The cables holding some of the screens were on fire.

"What's the point?" Niko said. "I'll be dead in a few days without the shelter."

You'll be dead in a few minutes if we stay here.

M-3 grabbed the cart and pulled it out of the corner. Niko helped push it through the debris to the steps. Isolated fires burned across the square where debris from the buildings had landed. The spider mechs that could walk were moving away, following the streets. One reached a dead end where a building had collapsed across it, blocking the way. It turned around, took a few steps along the street, then turned back and stepped toward the rubble. Then it turned away and repeated the movement, stuck in a loop as it tried to find a way out.

Niko helped M-3 carry the cart down the steps, then dragged the front between piles of flaming debris as M-3 pushed it from behind. One of the screens fell as the burning cables snapped, and it smashed on the ground. Sharp shards of burning plastic scattered around them.

They pushed and pulled the cart through the streets, between burning buildings, and past debris piles. One of the vehicles burst into a giant ball of flame as whatever ancient fuel was left inside ignited. They backed away, and dragged the cart to the side of of the street as more caught alight.

Broken stone blocks moved beside them. A gun-bot flicked its legs among the rubble. As they dragged the cart past, its legs found solid footings against a vehicle and piles of blocks. Its body rose from the ground. Motors whirred and its joints groaned as it turned toward the cart.

Crap.

The gun-bot swung around and the guns twisted in their direction. Bullets cracked through the air around them, and hammered into the debris. One ricocheted from M-3's side with a thunk. As M-3 pushed the cart behind the nearest vehicle, Niko dove to the ground. She grabbed rocks and threw them at the gun-bot.

Then a wall sloughed away from the tall, burning building behind. Chunks fell around them, smashing dozens of the alien vehicles. Niko yelped and covered her head.

And a chunk the size of the vehicles landed on the gun-bot. It sparked as it collapsed under the impact, and the guns fired the last of their ammunition into the air.

They stopped on the road outside the city, and watched it burn. The flames illuminated the night, turning the grey plain orange for hours until they had consumed whatever fuel and flammable materials remained. Thick smoke billowed into the air above them, rising kilometres into the sky, then blowing out in a stream toward the mountains.

"Sorry," M-3 said. It had only wanted to do the right thing, and now it had done this. It should have known better than to rush a repair, and bodge up a quick fix.

That was really fucking...

The SI stopped talking.

The reactor buzzed. M-3 checked the alarms.

Fuel exhausted. Reactor shutdown.

"Fuel gone," M-3 said.

Niko turned away from the flames and crossed her arms over her chest. Tears dripped down her cheeks behind the visor, reflecting the fire light. "That was really fucking... bad."

They waited in the dark, watching the last of the flames, until the sun rose. The fire had reduced most of the buildings to bare frames among smoking rubble. They had achieved more destruction in one day than nature had in centuries.

"Fire going," M-3 said. "Could go back."

Niko stood and brushed the grey dust from her suit. "Let's see what's left of the shelter. Maybe you can repair it for me, somehow."

M-3 took hold of the cart and began to push it toward the ruins. Niko put a paw on its manipulators.

"Leave that here. We'll move faster on our own."

"Can't abandon SI."

"No-one's going to come along and steal it. We can come back once we've sorted something out."

"What if don't come back?"

"Then it won't matter."

She lead the way back along the road, and M-3 tried to keep up. As she strode ahead, M-3 had to turn its sirens on every few minutes to warn her to stop and wait for it to catch up. Then, after a while, she stopped waiting and left M-3 behind.

Rain began to fall, thick, muddy rain washing the smoke out of the sky, and grey like the rest of the planet. M-3 forced its way through the hot rubble, looking for flames and using its infra-red sensors to avoid the remaining fires. Steam rose from the bare metal shells of the alien vehicles as the rain splattered on the surface and hissed as it boiled in the heat.

Niko was sitting on the soot-stained steps of the pyramid as M-3 reached the square. The shelter lay flat on the ground, blackened by the fire and torn by the spider mechs' feet. Her suit looked little better. It had protected her from the flames, but the silver surface was blistered and singed.

She looked up as M-3 approached. "I'm done."

M-3 scanned the area. All it could see was the burnt debris of the dead city, and the burnt bones of its inhabitants.

"Done what?"

"I've been stuck in that shelter for years. I've been stuck in this suit for hours. I can't spend the rest of my life in it."

"Try to repair shelter."

"I don't want to go back in there. I want to live in the open, without this damn suit."

She reached up to her helmet.

"Just reanimate my old self from the lifeboat store when the rescue arrives."

"No. Backup now. Will reanimate this instance."

M-3 could retrieve the brain scanner from the shelter and back her up before she died. It shouldn't take long if it could find a way to power the thing. She had no reason to lose this instance of herself.

"I don't want to remember any of this," she said, then reached to her neck to unclip the helmet from the suit.

She pulled the helmet off, and took a long, deep breath of the smokey, damp air.

CHAPTER SEVEN

"Why am I not dead?" Niko said, ten minutes later. She turned on the spot, surveying the burnt desolation around them. Then looked back at M-3. "Why didn't I die like Randolph?"

M-3 struggled through the debris to the burnt remains of the shelter. The walls had collapsed, and were now blackened, covered with soot and scattered stones. It grabbed the material with a primary manipulator and lifted it.

The apple tree lay underneath, dirt spilled from the box, leaves singed.

But still alive.

M-3 picked up the tree, moved concrete blocks out of the way, and placed it upright. It searched the leaves and trunk with its nanomanipulators. They were covered with a thin layer of soot and grey dust, but no nanoplague bots.

It stepped back, and pointed its manipulators at the tree.

"Plague gone."

Niko walked down the steps and crouched by the tree. She ran her gloved fingers over the leaves. "What do you mean, gone?"

"Not there. Tree clean."

"Ow," Niko said as M-3 pressed its manipulators against her suit. Then she giggled as the nanomanipulators removed the last of the plague bots from the exterior and disassembled them.

It only found about a dozen, on the clean spots between the soot. Nanoscale blobs of carbon were embedded in the blackened and blistered material between. The remains of the nanoplague bots that had been exposed to the flames.

"Plague burned."

"Fire? Why didn't we think of that?" She looked around them at the charred remains of the city. "Shame we had to burn down the whole place."

It did seem free of plague for now. M-3 examined the rest of the square and found very few plague bots which had not been burned to molten blobs, or damaged so badly that they would be unable to kill anything. It would need to find a way to stop them being blown back into the city from the plain outside. Perhaps it could build a shelter over the entire city. Or use the power from the hydro plant to create a wall of flames that would destroy any plague bots as they blew in. Once M-3 brought the SI back to the city and plugged it into the alien power supply, it would think of something.

Chunks of wall and ceiling blocked much of the entrance to the pyramid. M-3 pulled some away, then stopped as the debris above began to creak. It assembled supports for the rest, then dug out a gap large enough to squeeze inside. The interior walls had burned, exposing the cables running behind them. Most of the power cables were as burned as those that had held the screens, which were now shattered down below. But some were still intact.

The floor had collapsed. A metre or two still stood near the walls, enough for M-3 to make its way around the entrance, but the rest had fallen into the basement. It reached the cables, pulled a loose one out of the wall and tested it with its electrical sensors. Power was still going through. It could extract the cables from the walls, assemble any adaptors it required, and use them to power the SI and its own batteries.

It released the cable, and glanced down as it turned to move further around the room. A light flashed in the basement. It was M-3's own lights, reflecting from the shiny door of the vault, now smeared with streaks of soot from the fire.

And the door was open.

M-3 tested its weight on ceiling debris which lay like a ramp, with one end at ground level and the other on top of a pile of burned wood from the crates in the basement. It creaked, but held, and M-3 climbed down it into the basement.

The vault door was only open a few centimetres, but that was a few centimetres more than it had been open before. Wires sparked behind the electrical panel, which was blackened and melted. It must have burned after the power was restored, and unlocked the door.

M-3 dragged burned crates away from the door, scattering their contents across the floor as it did so. Then it went back and pushed everything else out of the way until there was room for the door to open.

"What are you doing?" Niko shouted.

She leaned over the edge of the big hole in the floor, now only wearing the gloves and boots from her suit and otherwise back in her normal clothes. M-3 turned so its lights illuminated the door.

"Oh," Niko said. "The door's open. Did you do that?"

M-3 slid its manipulators into the gap between the door and frame. It was still well sealed, but the gap was large enough to slide tertiary manipulators in to provide enough grip to pull the door open.

Rubble clattered down the ceiling panels behind it as Niko slid down on her ass. She stood beside M-3 and brushed the worst of the dust and soot off her clothes.

"Open it, then. I want to know what's in there before I die."

M-3 pulled. The door still resisted, and it strained as hard as it could to no avail. It pushed its manipulators further into the gap, until they stopped, the ends pressing against an obstruction inside. Something soft and rubbery.

It wiggled the manipulators until it opened a small gap in the seal. Air hissed faintly through the gap, and M-3 reached the far side of the door with the end of the manipulators. It pulled against the pressure difference, and hinges creaked and groaned as the door opened for the first time in centuries.

"What the hell are these things?" Niko said. She had opened one of the metal cases that lined the walls inside the vault, and removed a transparent container holding thousands of small spheres. She held it in front of M-3's sensors.

Looks like seeds, perhaps. This building appears to have been some kind of museum, they may have built this vault to store seed samples for the future.

M-3 had returned to the cart and dragged it into the city, then turned on power to the computer before it let Niko touch anything in the vault. It had learned its lesson with the whole burning-down-the-city experience, and would let the SI make the big decisions in future.

Niko shook the box. The spheres rattled against the interior. "What would they grow?"

How would I know? We'd have to plant some and see what sprouts. Of course, once the nanoplague returns here, they will all die.

"If it returns, I'll die."

Even if it doesn't, the plants may not be able to reproduce if they need flying animals to pollinate them as many known plants do.

"Could build micro-drones," M-3 said. They'd be able to do the job if they were programmed right.

"Growing plants will give me something to do until help gets here," Niko said.

M-3 opened another of the metal cases. Larger containers were packed inside, hundreds across each row, and dozens of rows from floor to ceiling. It slid one of the containers out. Many more layers were packed in behind.

It moved the container closer to its sensors so the SI could see the contents through the transparent walls. The container was packed full of small ovoids, each with six sticks poking out.

Very interesting. They look very much like miniature versions of the bodies we found in the city.

Niko leaned over M-3 and stared at the box. "Do you really think the aliens grew from seeds?"

Unlikely, but not unknown. We found animate plant life when we visited HD 96566 many years ago.

"So we could just plant them and they'd grow?"

It would certainly make an interesting experiment. Sentient life evolved from plants would be a very significant discovery, worth the trip here.

"Worth everyone dying?"

I'm sure they'll agree, after we reanimate them.

Niko tapped the side of the box. The seeds jiggled inside. "Plant-people still seem freaky to me."

Says the girl made from mixing human DNA with a cat.

"My family have been cats for centuries."

Besides, it's not much different to some organic planting a seed in you. It just finds sustenance in the soil instead of your body. What's more freaky about that than the way you organics already reproduce?

As Niko and the SI argued, M-3 turned the box around in its manipulators.

It had an idea.

CHAPTER EIGHT

The spider mech trudged along the worn and broken road on a bright, sunny day. A foot stuck in a long, narrow rut as it tried to move forward, and it stopped, pulling and twisting the foot until it broke free. It walked on ahead, moving slowly on battery power, with only two large solar panels on its back to recharge them.

It stepped off the road onto the grey dust. Gas hissed from vents cut into its underside, then igniters clicked. Sparks burst from them, flying into the gas. Flames flashed around the sparks, then the gas jets caught light. Long jets of flame blasted the ground beneath the mech as it crept across the dirt for a hundred metres, and arms fitted at the rear dug into the ground, burying the grey dirt of destroyed life, and exposing the soil beneath. Then it turned, moved three metres sideways, and crept back toward the road, clearing more ground.

M-3 watched the mech clear the area, then step back on the road and go into standby while the solar panels recharged the batteries. Not bad for a quick bodge job, and, this time, the new invention was supposed to burn things down. Repairing the wells and pipelines that provided the gas to the city had been another complex task, but the one thing it had plenty of was time. In comparison, replacing the mech's computer and then reprogramming it for the new job had been easy.

M-3 trudged into the seared patch, and scraped up a pile of dirt to examine with its nanomanipulators. The flames had burned up all the plague bots, then the arms churned up the ground and buried the remains. It could add containers on the arms, and modify them to deposit seeds in the freshly cleared dirt. With no animals to eat the seeds, they could all grow into plants.

There were hundreds of spider mechs still in the city, and many more outside where they had collapsed as they reached the limit of their transmitted power. It could build a huge mech army, transforming the instruments of the planet's destruction into its tools of repair.

Meanwhile, Niko was trying to grow aliens, back in the city. If they grew, the SI could use the remains of her suit to design protective suits for them, so they could travel across the planet, even into areas where the plague was still active. The mech army would grow as they found more and converted them. So long as they could find fuel for the gas jets, the mechs could work until their mechanical components failed beyond any hope of repair.

And there were still at least a thousand years before help would arrive.

Perhaps M-3 could repair the planet, after all.

AUTHOR'S NOTES

The working title of Fade To Grey was originally Final Contact 2, until I found a better one. It's almost a sequel to that story, set a short time after it, and looking at another way alien species might screw up their planet so humans end up colonizing the whole galaxy.

In the The Future universe, Luddites destroyed Earth many centuries ago, and here, the Luddites among the aliens went even further, leaving the planet intact, but destroying all life on it, so it might as well have been destroyed too.

Ultimately, I just liked the image of the spider mechs spreading destruction around the planet, then heading out again like alien Johnny Appleseeds, spreading the seeds that would return life to a dead world.

ABOUT THE AUTHOR

Edward M. Grant spent his childhood in the South-West of Britain and studied Physics at Oxford, but now lives in Canada. He wrote magazine articles and worked on numerous indie movies in and around London, including co-writing a vampire movie that was later shot in California. He has travelled the world, been a VIP at several space shuttle launches, survived earthquakes and a tsunami, climbed Mt Fuji and visits nuclear explosion sites as a hobby.

He grew up on pulp horror and SF novels and still has a soft spot for both. However, his background as a physicist helps him write stories toward the harder end of the SF spectrum.

Find him online at **www.edwardmgrant.com**.

Also By Edward M. Grant

WELCOME TO THE FUTURE

No-one expects to find alien life in NGC 2419. But when the first probes encounter a dirty, industrial planet somewhere no human is known to have been, the race is on to be the first to welcome its inhabitants into the galactic community. Will it be two poker-playing starships, or The Future, for whom pretension is a vocation, not just a way of life?

A 5,500 word science fiction short story.

FINAL CONTACT

Ever wondered where the aliens are? Bill is sure they don't exist, but after centuries searching the galaxy for any sign of intelligent life, I'm not about to give up yet.

I've just received this hot tip from a gang of Luddites out near M15. Hot enough that even Bill has chosen to join me for my final attempt to prove him wrong...

A 4,000 word science fiction short story set in The Future's universe.